TELL ME ANOTHER!

*A New Collection of After-Dinner Stories
from the House of Lords and the
House of Commons*

Compiled by Jack Aspinwall, MP

Foreword by George Thomas,
Viscount Tonypandy

Illustrated by David Mostyn

CENTURY

LONDON   MELBOURNE   AUCKLAND   JOHANNESBURG

Note:
In the course of the production of this book there have been a number of changes of Members' positions in the Houses of Parliament. While every effort has been made to keep up with these changes, it has, inevitably, not been possible to make all the necessary alterations.

First published in hardcover in 1986 by Century Hutchinson Ltd, Brookmount House, 62–65 Chandos Place, Covent Garden, London WC2N 4NW

Century Hutchinson Publishing Group (Australia) Pty Ltd, PO Box 496, 16–22 Church Street, Hawthorn, Melbourne, Victoria 3122, Australia

Century Hutchinson Group (NZ) Ltd, PO Box 40–086, Glenfield, Auckland 10

Century Hutchinson Group (SA) Pty Ltd, PO Box 337, Bergvlei 2012, South Africa

Reprinted 1986
First published in paperback in 1987

Set by Deltatype Lecru, Ellesmere Port, Cheshire

Printed in Great Britain by
Richard Clay Ltd, Bungay, Suffolk

ISBN 0 7126 1614 4

ABOUT THE AUTHOR

Jack Aspinwall was born in the North. He has been connected with voluntary caring work for many years. He founded and motivated many projects for the care of the elderly and for those less fortunate in society. In 1979 he was elected to Parliament to represent the constituency of Kingswood near Bristol, and in 1983 the constituency of Wansdyke. Mr Aspinwall has travelled widely and has been inspired to continue his work in the literary world after visiting Third World countries. Many charities have benefited from the proceeds of his books and will continue to do so.

Also available from Century in paperback

Kindly Sit Down! *Compiled by Jack Aspinwall*

FOREWORD
by
George Thomas,
Viscount Tonypandy

It is a delight and an honour to pen this Foreword for my good friend, Jack Aspinwall. Reading the pages of the manuscript has been an experience full of nostalgia, as well as laughter: It is as if I were back in the Speaker's Chair, looking over that unique assembly once again. Jack Aspinwall's collection, however, is much more entertaining than many a day in the Commons, for not only do you see household names on every page, but they then regale you with the best memories they have.

One memory I have, which goes back to my childhood, is of being a keen supporter of the National Children's Home, collecting for its wonderful work both at home and in the streets. Now, as Chairman, I marvel at the way the charity is addressing itself to every contemporary problem and need.

Last year NCH launched its Children in Danger Campaign for the increasing number of children exposed to real danger today – from poverty, homelessness and divorce, no less than from abduction, sexual abuse, violence and drugs. One of the campaign's first champions was Jack Aspinwall, who donated £5,000 from the proceeds of *Kindly Sit Down*! to NCH's Missing Link Project. This project aims to establish links with runaway children, by nationwide appeals and hi-tech monitoring, and to research the causes of this growing problem.

I know your pleasure will be sharpened by the knowledge that some of the proceeds of this book will go to NCH to help runaway children, and many other charities will benefit too.

George Tony pandy.

July 1986

DEDICATION

To Brenda, my wife, who continues to need her sense of humour.

To Viscount Tonypandy for kindly writing the Foreword.

To Margaret Thatcher for her fine example and encouragement.

To Sally, Jenny and Sarah for helping.

To Barbara and Madge for continuing to help to make it all happen.

To my parliamentary colleagues and friends for their support and contributions.

To all those generous souls who help others to make our world a better place in which to live – you know who you are!

To my friends in the Press and media who have generously written about, photographed, televized and broadcast endless cheque presentations and amusing incidents and anecdotes – thank you!

INTRODUCTION
by
Jack Aspinwall, MP

This is my third book of after-dinner stories – many of them prized possessions of my parliamentary colleagues and friends. I am eternally grateful for all the help which has been given to me.

Who would have thought that, when I was involved in a serious parachuting accident after a sponsored jump for charity, I would be able to produce bestselling books of after-dinner stories? First *Kindly Sit Down!*, then *Hit Me Again! (I Can Still Hear The Swine)*, and now *Tell Me Another!* – all written to raise funds for various charities.

Viscount Tonypandy (George Thomas), former Speaker of the House of Commons, has written the Foreword for this book, and I am indeed honoured. I remember an occasion in early 1985, when a much troubled constituent travelled to London with her little boy to see me. I had taken all the details of her case and started the process of helping, and thought that my constituent would like to look briefly around the Palace of Westminster. We eventually arrived at the House of Lords and there met Viscount Tonypandy to whom I introduced my constituent and her little boy. George (he won't mind if I call him that) in his typical caring and friendly way soon put my visitors at ease and delighted the little boy by giving him a one pound note. My friends from Wansdyke went home absolutely delighted! Some months later I was speaking at a lunch at the Travellers' Club in London at the invitation of the National Children's Home, and was able to tell George that he had indeed cast his bread on the waters when he gave my little friend from Wansdyke one pound, because now I was able to give him a cheque for £5,000 to help children in need – all from the proceeds of books like this one.

Many charities have benefited from my books. I recall attending a Chamber of Commerce dinner in Bristol and presenting H.R.H. Princess Anne with a substantial cheque for Save the Children Fund. I also gave her a copy of *Kindly Sit Down!* and was amused to hear from Her Royal Highness later that she wished she had received a copy of it before making her speech, rather than after!

A great highlight was an invitation to supper at Buckingham Palace from Her Majesty the Queen. You can imagine the great thrill and excitement that prevailed for my wife, Brenda, and me! Both of us went through the protocol and conventions of how to do things correctly – to call Her Majesty the Queen 'Your Majesty', first of all when spoken to, and thereafter 'Ma'am'. All this was carefully rehearsed. Then the opportunity came to meet Her Majesty, and I was asked which area I represented as a Member of Parliament. Recalling that my constituency name sounded like the name of an English cheese, when asked, in my fluster I said 'Lymeswold'! Of course, it should have been 'Wansdyke'. My remarks produced great royal amusement!

Tim Yeo, MP

As a newly elected Member of Parliament, completely unknown to the world, I was naturally keen to make my mark and above all to be noticed by the Prime Minister at an early stage.

I observed that during Question Time, when answering questions herself, she had to concentrate very carefully on her own answers and therefore only had limited attention for her questioner. Each Tuesday and Thursday, however, there was a vital five minutes or so when she came into the House and was sitting on the Front Bench listening to the end of the departmental questions which preceded her own period at 3.15 pm.

This appeared to me to be the optimum time since she could observe the questioners closely as another Minister would be giving the answer.

Accordingly one afternoon, when I happened to be sitting next to another new Member, Mr Francis Maude, I decided to put my plan into action. The Prime Minister came into the House at about seven minutes past three and took her seat on the Front Bench where a senior Minister, since retired, was answering questions.

I seized my chance and hopped up. To my great delight the Speaker called me. I preceded to ask my carefully rehearsed question, and sat down to enquire of my neighbour what effect it had had.

He told me that my plan had worked brilliantly in part, but failed in another part.

Apparently after I asked my question the Prime Minister leant to the senior Minister by her side, and said to him

'Who is that extremely intelligent new young Member?' When my neighbour told me this, I felt that my career was well on its way.

Unfortunately, however, the Minister had then turned around and taken a long look at me and then turned back to the Prime Minister and said: 'Oh yes, I know him, his name is Francis Maude.'

I believe that this incident was the main reason why Francis Maude was soon promoted to the Whips Office and I languished on the backbenches.

Norman Lornie
Parliamentary Affairs Officer British Airways

Harry Hynd, MP, retired now for some years, used to relate the story of the old Argyllshire minister who typified that local familiarity with the Almighty and the laird alike, by regularly praying aloud with his congregation for those afflicted by some local misfortune, saying: 'Oh Lord, as Thou will have read in last week's *Oban Times*. . . .'

Cyril D. Townsend, MP

At the Queen's Coronation, the giant Queen Salote of Tonga was accompanied in her open carriage by a tiny man in a bowler hat and pin-stripe trousers.

Someone asked Noël Coward, who was watching, who the little man was.

Replied Noël Coward, 'Her Lunch!'

The Rt Hon. Gregor Mackenzie, MP

Two Ministers of the Crown and their wives were on holiday on the Isle of Skye. One day they decided to go for a drive, but sadly a thick mist came down. Very sensibly they stopped and decided to wait until they could find out exactly where they were before driving on. They waited and they waited. Eventually they heard the clumps of boots on the road. The Minister who had been driving the car wound down the window and asked the walker, a shepherd, where they were. 'You are in your motor car,' came the reply. Not unreasonably, the Minister was a bit annoyed until his colleague said, 'That is the very model of a parliamentary answer. It is brief, it is true and it doesn't tell you anything you don't already know.'

Roger Moate, MP

Businessmen are often told that exporting is fun! But they well know that it involves extensive and arduous trips abroad, long periods of separation and many hazards.

One such businessman was at home in bed when there

was a great flash of lightning which lit up the room. To the astonishment of his wife he leapt out of bed crying, 'I'll buy the negative – I'll buy the negative!'

Lord Harmer-Nicholls, Bt, JP

Gratitude is short term:

The general public's capacity for retaining feelings of gratitude was exemplified by the experience of an American senator, who visited an erstwhile keen supporter and said. . . .

'John, I hear you're not going to support me in my next election.'

'No, Senator, I am not.'

'But you remember when I was first elected and was able to help your brother with his business problem, you said how impressed you were.'

'That's right, Senator, I was.'

'Then when your son had his domestic trouble, I was able to be of some assistance.'

'That's right, Senator, you were.'

'And then don't forget when you fell foul of bureaucracy, I intervened to some purpose.'

'Yes, that's right, Senator, you did – but what have you done for me recently?'

5

Dafydd Wigley, MP

The only parliamentary incident worth a smile during the last twelve months was when I accidentally dislodged the arm from the Speaker's Chair during a rather heated exchange with Harold Walker, when the Unborn Children's Bill was being discussed. After the furore, when I left the Chamber for the Members' Lobby, I was besieged by every press person in Westminster. I tried to explain away what I had done – rather clumsily as it happened – I told them 'There was a loose screw in the chair.' Mercifully, the Press asked me to clarify before they printed any suggestions that it was a comment on the Deputy Speaker himself!

Gary Waller, MP

'I hear you're going on the stage.'
'Yes, I've just landed the part of Long John Silver.'
'Really? How much are they paying you?'
'Two thousand pounds a week. I start on Tuesday.'
'Two thousand! I'd start on *Monday* for two thousand!'
'Can't do that. I'm having my leg off on Monday.'

Later. . . .

'How's the pantomime going?'
'Great. They've given me a part in Peter Pan as well now.'
'That sounds wonderful.'

'Yes, except I had to have my hand off and wear a hook. Oh, and I lost an eye.'
'Good God! How'd you lose the eye?'
'A pigeon flew over and scored a direct hit.'
'I've never heard of anyone losing an eye that way!'
'You do if you forget you've got a hook.'

Christopher Chope, OBE, MP

Have you heard about the lengths to which the Taiwanese will go in business? An English wholesaler ordered a quantity of crockery but, nervous about the reference to countries of origin, he specified that there should not be any mention of it being manufactured in Taiwan. The consignment of crockery duly arrived with the imprint on the base of each item, 'Not made in Taiwan'.

A. Cecil Walker, JP, MP

An inmate of an asylum appeared before the board requesting his discharge from the institution on the grounds that he was no longer insane.

'What would be the first thing you'd do if we discharged you?' he was asked.

'I'd make a catapult (slingshot) and break every window in this place,' he replied.

Of course, the petition was denied and he was put back in his cell.

The next year he again appealed for a discharge.

'What would be the first thing you'd do if we let you out,' he was asked. 'I'd make a catapult and break every window in this place,' was the answer.

Finally upon his sixth appeal, the usual question was put to him and he answered, 'I'd make a date with my girl Maggie.'

The Committee perked up. Well, they thought, this sounds like something a little different. Perhaps now we'll get somewhere.

'What would you do on this date?' he was asked.

'Well,' he replied, 'I'd hire a car and take Maggie for a drive out into the woods, making sure it was dark.'

'And then?'

'Then I'd stop the car and make love to her.'

'And then?'

'And then I'd sneak my hand up her dress.'

'And?'

'Then I'd pull off her girdle, tear out the elastic, make me a nice big catapult, and come back here and break every darned window in the place.'

Cranley Onslow, MP
Chairman of 1922 Committee

An American, newly posted to Brussels, the story goes, has difficulty in defining a European. He is promptly enlightened. A European is someone who has:

The ability to work as hard as the English;
The sobriety of the Irish;
The modesty of the French;
The broad horizons of the Luxemburger;
The prudishness of the Danes;
The humour of the Germans;
The generosity of the Dutch;
The real sense of the Italians;
The patience of the Greeks;
In other words – he is a Belgian.

Terence Brooks
Formerly working in Palace of Westminster

Before Harold Macmillan became the Earl of Stockton he came to the House of Lords. The constable who received him said brightly, 'Good morning, Sir Harold.' 'No, my boy, that's the other fellah,' (Harold Wilson) said Mr Macmillan. The officer apologetically said, 'Sir, you've such an air about you that one's tempted to give you a titled address.' 'I turned that down too,' came the reply.

Neil Thorne, OBE, TD, MP

When a chicken and a pig were travelling together and stopped for breakfast, the pig declined the offer of bacon and egg because to the chicken it was but a contribution, but to him it was a total commitment.

Paddy Ashdown, MP

A little anecdote to be spoken with a West Country accent and which is also somewhat onomatopoeic . . .

My wife and I were out walking some time ago in the rather beautiful collection of hills around Buckland St Mary. We were new to the area, at the time (about fifteen years ago) and due to meet some friends in the village. We had got ourselves slightly lost in the tangle of lanes, as I judged it, about a mile from the village. We were concerned about missing our appointment and so stopped to ask a farmer leaning over a gate how long it would take us to get to Buckland St Mary. He uttered what I took at the time to be merely a rather rude sound which sounded like 'Waak'. I thought this was the common hospitality shown in the area to the visitors, but to make sure asked him the question again. I got the same response. At this stage my wife and I decided that we should continue the journey, unadvised. We had taken no more than ten paces when I heard the voice behind me saying 'Ten Minutes'. I turned round in perplexity. My farmer friend said "Ow cin oi tell 'eee 'ow long it will take 'eee to git to Buckland St Mary til oi see 'ow faast 'eee cin waak!'

Sir Peter Emery, MP

Something I heard on a British Caledonian flight from Los Angeles to Gatwick:

The public address system, as landing cards are being taken around for passengers, announces: 'Landing cards are necessary for all passengers other than those with British passports or members of the EEC.'

An air hostess approaches, a crass American businessman demands: 'Gee – I'm not a member; Give me an application form – I must join this EEC!'

Nicholas R. Winterton, MP

The Duke of Wellington, while reviewing his troops before Waterloo, is reputed to have said, 'I don't know what effect these men may have on the enemy, but by God, they frighten me!'

Peter Viggers, MP

An ecumenical conference was organized, to take place in Paris, and three preachers from the Welsh Valleys were

11

included in the group. As their plane turned over Paris on its final approach one of the preachers turned to his two colleagues and said: 'As we are to be together for a week here in Paris I feel I can let you into a secret. Nobody knows at home, but I have a vice which I am longing to exercise while I am here. It is women. I can't keep my hands off them. I am told that the Parisian girls are very lovely, and I can't wait to get to the city and find out for myself.'

The second preacher said: 'Since you have been so frank I will admit that I too have a vice. It is drink. I like the beer well enough in Wales but I am looking forward to the French wine and strong brandy and I can't wait to get into the first bar.'

The third preacher was silent for a moment then he spoke: 'I too have a vice; it is an unpleasant thing to confess and in many ways it is nastier and more anti-social than either of your problems.' His two colleagues looked at him in wonder and then he went on 'My vice is gossip . . . and I can't wait to get back to the Welsh Valleys to tell our colleagues what I have just heard.'

A. Cecil Walker, JP, MP

A well-known rakish MP said to a lovely young blonde in the Commons Bar, 'If I'd ask you to become my secretary at £200 per week, would you say "Yes".'

'A dozen times a day, if necessary.'

Tim Sainsbury, MP

Q.E.D.:
Three men, a chemist, a carpenter and an economist, were shipwrecked on a desert island. It was barren, and their only means of support was an enormous tin of corned beef. But the tin had arrived without an opener.

The chemist, with great self-confidence, told the other two not to worry: 'I will distil an acid from the island's minerals and corode the top of the tin.'

The carpenter said that would be too slow. 'Let me forage for sticks and stones, make a hammer and smash the can.'

The economist sighed and raising his eyes to the sun began ... 'That's too crude. Let us assume a tin-opener. . . .'

Sir Kenneth Lewis, DL, MP

The difference between men and boys
Is simply the size of their toys!

John A. Wilson
External Relations Executive, British Aerospace PLC

Some years ago when my children were very young, I achieved the professional status of Chartered Engineer and there was the usual degree of polite congratulations within the family. My young children obviously did not understand the whole affair but they did listen. On the evening after the news came through, my wife was listening to my four-year-old daughter saying her prayers and in particular the Lord's Prayer which went thus:

'Our father, Chartered in Heaven!'

Norman Lornie
Parliamentary Affairs Officer British Airways

A story told to me by Bob Hughes MP when showing some MPs around the helicopter base in support of North Sea Oil:

The good citizens of Aberdeen took to the oil boom with enthusiasm and it must be said – they say it themselves – that a certain amount of commercial exploitation of the flood of incoming American oilmen was not unknown. Mr Hughes said he spent much of his time suggesting to his constituents that the long-term benefits of oil to the Aberdeen economy were potentially considerable, and in one talk to an elderly Aberdonian constituent he remarked:

'Why, Willie, there's oil out there for another hundred years . . .' To which the old chap replied: 'Aye. I knew it wouldna last . . .'

Gerald Howarth, MP

Ill wind:

Mr Brown knew none of the facts of life, only the facts of making money. Having done that, he decided to try pigfarming, and bought a prize sow. Assured that a mating with the neighbouring farmer's boar, for a modest fee, would produce piglets, he put his sow in a wheelbarrow and rushed her round to the boar.

To Brown's chagrin, he being a man used to instant results, there were no piglets when he looked next morning. So, deciding that this was no time to quibble over money, he put the sow in the wheelbarrow and hurried her to the local squire's champion boar, paid a higher fee and went home again.

Next morning, still no piglets.

So Brown decided to pay the top price for Britain's best boar, who was luckily living nearby. It was into the wheelbarrow again and a very large cheque changed hands for the services of this infallible boar.

Next morning he rushed to the sow's pen, agog. Alas, no piglets. But the sow was sitting in the wheelbarrow.

Geoffrey Dickens, JP, MP

A very ugly woman asked me for an autograph at a summer fête I had opened. Certainly – if you care to drop me a note at the House of Commons I will be delighted to send you a photograph, I volunteered. Four weeks later a charming letter arrived from that lady and after her signature she had bravely written Horseface in brackets. Filled with admiration for the way in which she had come to terms with her repulsive looks, I entered into the spirit of things. With a felt-tipped pen I wrote on the photograph 'To My Dear Friend Horseface – Love and Best Wishes, Geoffrey Dickens.' After it was safely in the post and on the way to my courageous constituent, my secretary informed me that she had been extremely helpful in writing Horseface after her name on the letter in case I had forgotten the lady in question.

Lord James Douglas-Hamilton, MA, LLB, MP

Lord Halifax in the seventeenth century said, 'Lawyers should be elected to Parliament only with so much circumspection that it would not happen very often.'

Hugh Dykes, MP

Often things are completely distorted or lost when messages or stories are passed on by word of mouth and they can completely change in meaning. Of course, this can be even worse when translating into different languages via interpreters, even the highly skilled operators who interpret in the United Nations or the European Parliament in Strasbourg.

This then gets even more complicated as the translation is not merely between two languages but passes through two, three, four or even more tongues.

So it was on one famous occasion when the interpreter who normally did Greek to Danish and Dutch had to stand in for a sick colleague and do the English from an Irish MEP. In his lengthy speech the MEP quoted the sayings, 'The Spirit is willing but the flesh is weak' and 'Out of sight, out of mind'.

They were translated finally as 'The whisky's all right here but the meat is awful' and 'The invisible idiot'!!

The Rt Hon. Lord Caccia, GCMG, GCVO

On hearing the anguished cries of children in the street, one of Abraham Lincoln's neighbours rushed out of his house in alarm. There he found Abraham Lincoln with his two sons, both sobbing uncontrollably. 'Whatever is the matter with the boys, Mr Lincoln?' he asked. 'Just what's the matter with the whole world,' replied Lincoln resignedly, 'I've got these three walnuts, and each wants two of them.'

Gary Waller, MP

'How old are you, Granny?' asked the four-year-old.

'Well, dear,' answered her grandmother coyly, 'I just can't remember my age.'

After a few moments thought, back came the helpful suggestion, 'Why don't you look in your knickers? Mine say four to five years old.'

Hon. Grenville Janner, QC, MP

My father, Barnett, was Labour MP for Leicester West for twenty-five years. Shortly before the 1970 election, he fell ill and was warned by his doctor that if he went electioneering, there could be no guarantee that he would survive the ordeal. So at the age of seventy-nine, he retired. As I had still not got a seat to fight, I joined the queue of would-be candidates and, after fierce contest, was selected.

My father delighted in the marvellous legend, almost universally believed: that he carefully retired six weeks before the election, when all posters and pamphlets had been printed with: 'Janner for Labour' – and as the local party could not afford a reprint, they had no alternative other than to select me!

My father then transferred his talents, not least as a raconteur, from the Commons to ten happy years in the Lords. Among his favourite remarks were the following:

At the start of a speech: 'As King Henry VIII said to each of his wives in turn – I shall not keep you long. . . .'

Fatherly love: 'I have never raised my hand to my son – except in self-defence!'

Michael Colvin, MP

Idiot-proof systems are no match for system-proof idiots.

Sir John Osborn, MP

When is a Member of Parliament a Spy?

There are always MPs who wish to pursue their hobbies or sports when attending international conferences, and the Interparliamentary Union Conference in 1980 in East Berlin proved to be no exception.

One MP, from Britain, drove to the Palast Hotel in West Berlin with the intention of swimming, playing tennis and some golf, as well as going sight-seeing. Although he arranged some international tennis at a small club in East Berlin, playing a game of golf proved to be more difficult.

To get from East Berlin to West Berlin involved a bus ride across Check-point Charlie, a trip on the metro, and a taxi to the famous golf course of Wallensee, now described as the American Services Sports Social and Golf Club.

Thinking about getting back to his hotel, in the bar at the 19th he enquired about taxis. 'The German cabs never come. The journey takes so long that most of those who have ordered them find some other means of getting back to barracks before the cab arrives. The cab drivers have got used to this so they now save themselves the trouble of coming.'

The MP had no problem in negotiating a lift back to the metro station with a drinking companion, until he indicated that he would be going back across Check-point Charlie. American forces are warned to take great care over whom they befriend. On the second round of drinks, the MP found himself challenged as being the most sophisticated spy yet out of East Berlin. Surely he was too British to be genuine?

The last Allied bus to cross Check-point Charlie was not long off. If the MP was to get back to the Palast Hotel (and not get taken for being the most *un*sophisticated spy out of West Berlin), he would have to think fast. He challenged, in fine statesman-like tones, 'Arrest me if you like, but you'd better be certain you can make the charge stick.'

Richard Ottaway, MP

The Duchess returned to the Manor one evening and encountered her butler in her boudoir. She looked the butler straight in the eye and said:

'James take off my dress.' James took off her dress.

'James take off my petticoat.' James took off her petticoat.

'James take off my bra.' James took off her bra.

'James take off my panties.' James took off her panties.
The Duchess turned, faced her butler again and in a soft but
firm voice said:

'Now then James, never let me catch you wearing my
clothes again.'

Michael Mates, MP

Dress rehearsal for the Sovereign's Parade on a snow-
covered square at Sandhurst. The band is playing, and the
adjutant on his charger is inspecting the cadets.

A snowball projected from somewhere in the ranks
strikes the charger on the quarters. The adjutant, unmoved,
shouts, 'Take his name, Sergeant-Major.' 'Got 'im, Sir,'
replies the RSM on the instant. 'Take his name, Drill
Sergeant.' 'Got 'im, Sir,' shouts the Drill Sergeant without
hesitation. 'Take that Gentleman Cadet to the Guardroom.'
'Got 'im, Sir,' reply two NCOs in unison and a cadet is
doubled away, feet barely touching the ground.

When the adjutant comes to inspect the band his steely
eye notices that the bass drummer only has one drumstick.
Upon enquiring why, the drummer answers, 'The woollen
head of the drumstick flew off some minutes ago as I was
twirling it. I'm afraid I did not see where it went.'

Tony Speller, MP

Speaking in the USA about the possibility of a woman President. 'I have no problem in accepting women in charge of men. After all, in Britain we are used to being ruled by women, the Queen, Margaret Thatcher and my wife – but not necessarily in that order!'

The late John Spence, MP

Repair bill for Church property found in a clock at Winchester Cathedral. The bill was drawn up in 1673:

To work done

	s	d
Oiling and repairing St Joseph	0	8
Oiling and ornamenting the Holy Spirit	0	6
Repairing the Virgin Mary before and behind and making a new child	4	8
Screwing a nose on the Devil – putting a horn on the tail and glueing a piece on his fork	5	6
TOTAL	11	4

A. Cecil Walker, JP, MP

A sure sign that social barriers no longer exist is the way so many ladies' maids enter a wealthy home by the servants' entrance and come out in a family way.

John M. Taylor, MP

Whilst travelling overseas with a Parliamentary delegation I wanted to call home. What follows is an impressive, if frustrating, exposition of modern technology when I tried to ring Solihull. I spoke into this smart phone at Vancouver Airport, asked if I could use my credit card and was answered most politely and told that I could. I gave its serial number and also the phone number I wanted to call and within seconds I was through to Solihull across 6,000 miles and eight time zones. A voice answered clearly enough. It was mine! I was through to my answering machine!

Michael Colvin, MP

The Liberals' Lament – with apologies to Anthony Delius:
Ten little Liberals trying to align,

Only one did so – and then there were nine.

Nine little Liberals entered a debate,
But one spoke his heart out – and then there were eight.

Eight little Liberals saw the road to Heaven,
One tried to follow it – and then there were seven.

Seven little Liberals trying hard to mix,
One got all mixed-up – and then there were six.

Six little Liberals eager to survive,
One turned a somersault – and then there were five.

Five little Liberals found they had the floor,
One spoke for all of them – and then there were four.

Four little Liberals sitting down to tea,
One choked on a principle – and then there were three.

Three little Liberals looking at the view,
One saw a policy – and then there were two.

Two little Liberals politically outrun,
One lost deposit – and then there was one.

One little Liberal found nothing could be done,
So he took the bus to Limehouse – and then there were none.

The Hon. Greville Janner, QC, MP

Taking sides:
    A tourist in Whitehall asked a policeman: 'Which side is the Foreign Office on?'

The officer replied: 'I understand, Sir, that it is meant to be on the side of the United Kingdom. But I sometimes wonder. . . .'

Sir Kenneth Lewis, DL, MP

Mum and small daughter were on a bus and the small girl was biting her nails. Mother pointed to a very fat man on this bus and said, 'You'll get like that if you keep biting your nails, my girl!'

A little later a rather pregnant lady got on the bus. The girl kept staring at her and as she came off the bus said to the lady, 'I know what you've been up to!'

S. T. Fahm

Ernest Bevin said to the War Cabinet:

At this time someone in the Ministry of Labour and National Service (not Mildred Riddelsdell) decided to go out to a Labour Exchange and conduct for herself the first call-up interview of any married woman. So Miss Smith from the Ministry Headquarters at 8 St James's Square went down to Tooting Labour Exchange and was soon in a private booth with the particulars of a Mrs Jones, who was shown in by a clerk.

'Do sit down,' said Miss Smith. 'We just want to have a

27

friendly talk. You know that we need every hand that we can get to help us with this dreadful war? Now let us see if you can help. I see here that you are married, aged thirty-five?' 'Yes, Miss.' 'In good health and no dependents?' 'That's so, Miss.' 'No children, I see?' 'No Miss.' 'What does your husband do Mrs Jones?'

Mrs Jones seemed a bit taken aback, blushed a bit but spoke up bravely. 'Oh we do all the usual things and we do it ever so often and at all times of the month. We've tried all those different positions they tell you about in books, Miss. We just do not have children. . . .'

Derek Conway, MP

Master Henry Conway aged three commented on the arrival of the latest addition to the family Conway, 'The baby has Mummy's eyes, Daddy's nose and MY flipping room!'

John Browne, MS, MBA, MP

A few years ago Britain played host to that magnificent man, His Holiness the Pope. As he stepped from the aeroplane and, as is customary, kissed the ground of England, a member of the welcoming delegation turned to my friend. He said, 'Why on earth does the Pope kiss the filthy dirty tarmac of Gatwick Airport?' My friend turned to him and as quick as a flash replied, 'Wouldn't you if you had flown Air Italia!'

Sir William Clark, MP

During the 1945–50 Parliament a Conservative Member, during an all-night sitting, said to his friends in the smoke room 'What are they talking about in the Chamber?' One friend said 'purchase tax', whereupon the Tory Member said he must make a speech. His friends tried to dissuade him, but to no avail, and the Member started to make his way towards the Chamber. One of his friends however, preceeded him, saw the Speaker, said that the Member was coming and that it would be a kindness not to call him. Eventually the Member arrived, sat himself on the Tory benches and waited for the Labour backbencher to finish his speech. He then leapt up and, as he was the only one standing on the Tory side, the Speaker had no option but to call him. He started off with great aplomb about the iniquities of purchase tax, how it would affect his constituents and how it was thoroughly reprehensible of the Government.

He then went on, 'and, moreover, Mr Speaker; moreover, Mr Speaker. . . .' it was here his memory failed him and he just forgot what he wanted to say. After about the seventh 'moreover, Mr Speaker' the Speaker leaned forward to consult the Clerk of the House as to the procedure where a Member obviously could not continue speaking but was still on his feet. Quick as a flash the Member, seeing the

Speaker talking to the Clerk, said 'Moreover, Mr Speaker, if you are not prepared to listen I am not prepared to tell you.' He then sat down and later rejoined his friends in the smoke room.

Michael Colvin, MP

The only person who got all his work done by Friday was Robinson Crusoe.

Jim Craigen, MLitt, FBIM, JP, MP

A veteran Irish politician, when asked the difference between Fianna Fáil and Fine Gael, replied, 'Let's put it this way – them that know don't need to ask and them that don't, don't need to know.'

Sir Kenneth Lewis, DL, MP

If you drink too much you go to sleep,
And when you sleep you cannot sin
If you do not sin you go to heaven
So, let us all drink!

Norman Lornie
Parliamentary Affairs Officer British Airways

Politicians and public figures may well care to ponder the story of the death of Franco. Surrounded on his deathbed by his faithful generals, he heard outside, beyond the heavily drawn curtains, a strange subdued noise like the sea, and asked someone to investigate. An aide did. He looked down from the palace balcony and returned with a lump in his throat and tears in his eyes and reported: 'Caudillo, it is the people. Thousands of them. They have come to say goodbye.' And Franco raised himself on one elbow and barked: 'Why? Where are they going?'

Lord Orr-Ewing, OBE

A keen follower of Rugby football recently met a 6′ 4″ Fijian, who had been prominent in their recent tour of Britain.

The sportsman said: 'We associate Fiji with waving palms, grass skirts, quiet beaches and calm blue sea. How is it you are so large and tough?'

The Fijian replied: 'You could say Rugby football is in my blood.'

'How come?'

'You see, my great-grandmother once ate a British second row forward!'

The Rt Hon. Gregor Mackenzie, MP

When motor buses were first introduced into London there was a lot of controversial discussion about them. Rumour has it that one rich and powerful peer of the realm stood in front of the fireplace of his London club and told anyone who was willing to listen how strongly he was opposed to them. However, one of his friends told him that before decrying them so loudly, he ought to dismiss his carriage and go home by bus. He agreed. He went out, got on to the first bus he saw, handed the conductor a sovereign and said '60 Eaton Square.' The reply is not recorded.

Lord Mancroft, KBE, TD

The phone at our local hospital rang in the early hours of the morning and the call was taken by George, our night duty operator.

'Hullo,' said George in his customary courteous way. An unknown caller said, 'Have you any adreno-cortecor-trophic-hormone in acqueous solution?'

'Eh?', said George.

The caller repeated his request, this time a little more slowly.

'Mister,' said George, 'When I said hullo I told you everything I know.'

Gary Waller, MP

'Trade's bad, Paddy, I think I'll sell the pub and start a brothel.'

'That'll not work, Seamus. If you can't sell beer, do you think you'll sell soup?'

A. Cecil Walker, JP, MP

At an exclusive private mental sanatorium the doctors and nurses were having a lot of trouble with two patients who both thought they were Napoleon Bonaparte. Every day during the exercise period the two of them would meet, start arguing and end up in a fight. A visiting psychiatrist was told of the problem and he suggested that the two patients be locked together in a room for a week, to give them time to convince one another. This was done, and for a week the two patients received only food and clean clothes from the outside. At the end of the week they were released and the head doctor approached one of them and asked 'Now, my friend. Do you still think you are Napoleon Bonaparte?'

'Well,' the patient answered, 'for quite some time now, I thought I really WAS Napoleon, but after a week with that other fellow, he's convinced me I'm Josephine!'

Robert A. McCrindle, MP

As one close to the travel industry, this is a collection of quotations from various foreign holiday brochures:

If this is your first visit to our hotel you are welcome to it.

You will not be likely to forget quickly your experience with us. Situated in the shadiest part of town, you cannot fail to remark from the window the odours of the pine trees and our swimming pool.

If you wish for breakfast, lift the telephone, ask for room service, and this will be enough for you to bring your food up.

On gala nights the chef throws his best dishes, and all water used in cooking has been passed by the manager personally.

If your wife needs something to do, she should apply to our suggestive head porter, but all of our staff are courteous, and to ladies too attentive.

We would very much like to have relations with you, and we will be most happy to dispose of all your clients.

Ian Mikardo, MP

Two Christian martyrs stood in the arena of the Coliseum in Ancient Rome, facing the ferocious, ravening lions who were about to be loosed on them. Said one to the other,

'Well, brother, we've got at least one consolation: there won't be a pitch invasion by the fans.'

A. Cecil Walker, JP, MP

The village drunk had passed out on a park bench. The little boy was playing nearby, making loud noises and shouting at the top of his voice.

'Go away kid . . .' he growled, 'go play somewhere else!'

'Ah, shut up' the kid answered, 'my old man says I can play wherever I want to.'

'Beat it, brat,' the drunk retorted, 'I'm trying to sleep.'

'Oh Yeah? Well my old man, when he's gotta sleep, he sleeps in bed!'

'Is that so – well he didn't sleep enough!'

Kenneth Warren, MP

When the Select Committee on Trade and Industry, during its review of UK Tourism, visited Northern Ireland in 1985, it was taken on a trip on an underground river soon to be opened to tourists. When the police escort were asked why they were shining torches down into the water, they replied, 'We're looking for enemies!'

To this the Chairman, Kenneth Warren, replied: 'You don't need to worry, Irish frogmen can't swim. They walk on the bottom!'

Cyril D. Townsend, MP

Some small children were being shown pictures of Christians in the Lions' Den by their teacher.

One tiny girl started crying and the teacher comforted her by saying that the Christians were on their way to heaven.

But this had no effect on the tiny girl who finally sobbed. 'But one little lion has not got a Christian!'

The Rt Hon. Lord Shackleton, KG, PC, OBE

Some years ago I was in Australia, and had trouble over a tooth which involved me going to a dentist and having a cap fitted. At the time, I was Leader of the Opposition in the House of Lords, and Earl Jellicoe was Leader of the House of Lords. In, I think, Sydney, Earl Jellicoe was given a State Dinner at which the Premier of New South Wales was present. At any rate, Earl Jellicoe, at the conclusion of his speech, said, 'I have a very serious complaint to make, the Australians have been interfering in British politics. They have been putting teeth into the Opposition.'

The Hon. Grenville Janner, QC, MP

Interviewing potential research assistants is a recurrent joy.

I was curious to know how an applicant had read about my vacancy. At the end of the interview, I asked him: 'How did you find me?'

Quick as a flash, he replied: 'Absolutely charming!'

At the end of another session with a young American aspirant, I said: 'Now, have you any questions for me?'

'Just one,' he said, 'Do you still play tennis?'

'Tennis?' I exclaimed, having never been much good at the game and not having played it for about three decades. 'What makes you think that I was a tennis player?'

'I read in *Who's Who* that in 1955, you contested Wimbledon!'

I had indeed – and lost by 12,000 votes.

Nicholas Baker, MP

The West Indies were playing Australia and the batsman, Redpath, was scoring runs freely. On receiving a short ball outside the offstump from one of the West Indian bowlers, Redpath went down on one knee and swept the ball from outside the offstump to the leg boundary amid Australian jubilation.

One of the highly knowledgeable West Indian supporters could take this no longer.

'Redpath,' he shouted, 'there are only three people in the world who can play that shot. Denis Compton, Everton Weekes and Frank Worrell. Redpath, you are an imposter!'

Tim Sainsbury, MP

Jonathan Sayeed, MP for Bristol East, was driving up the motorway to Bristol early one Saturday. As he was late for his Advice Centre, the speed at which he was travelling caught the attention of a police car.

'Are you aware, Sir, of how fast you are driving?' asked the officer.

'I am sorry, Officer, I'm afraid I am late for my surgery,' was the unpremeditated reply.

'In that case, Doctor,' said the policeman magnanimously, 'Drive on. We can't keep all those sick people waiting, can we.'

Barry Sheerman, MP

After a particularly long speech in 1979, someone said to me, 'I'll say the same to you as I used to say to Hugh Gaitskell, "You can tell you were a university lecturer, you can only speak for fifty minutes." '

A. Cecil Walker, JP, MP

A young lovely was having her house painted and when she got up one morning she noticed a spot where her husband had leaned against the door frame.

She called downstairs to the painter, 'Would you come up here a minute? I'd like to show you where my husband put his hand last night.'

'If it's all the same to you, lady,' he replied, 'I'll just settle for a glass of beer.'

Barry Sheerman, MP

An older Member who put his arm round me when I first entered Parliament and was complaining about the number of letters to answer said, 'I have been in this House since 1945 and I have one golden rule. Never answer letters, it only encourages them.'

Colin Shepherd, MP

Baby Polar Bear: 'Mummy, am I a polar bear?'
Mummy Polar Bear: 'Yes, of course, darling.'

Baby Polar Bear:	'Are you sure I am a Polar bear? Are you sure I am not a brown bear?'
Mummy Polar Bear:	'Good gracious me, of course you're not a brown bear, whatever gave you that idea?'
Baby Polar Bear:	'Because I'm cold!'

Tim Smith, MP

The Fayed brothers were inspecting Harrods prior to purchase. They were introduced to Harrods' Salesman of the Year. What, they inquired, had he done to achieve such an award?

'Well,' he said, 'I sold a gentleman a fishing rod. And then I said to him, if you are going fishing, you will need the rest of the tackle, a line, flies, waders, waterproof clothing and a hat. These he readily agreed to buy. Then I said to him, you must have one of our excellent hampers for your picnic lunch. So I sold him one. Then I asked him, what are you going to put all this gear in? Would you like to buy a truck? He was persuaded at once. So I inquired how he was going to get to Scotland, and following some further discussion I sold him a car.'

The Fayed brothers were impressed. 'The Sports Department must have been delighted with your success.' they said.

'I work in the pharmacy,' replied the salesman.

'In the pharmacy?' they exclaimed.

'Yes,' he said, 'you see, this man came in and said, "I'm going away for the weekend with my wife and I would like

to buy some Tampax." "Oh," I said, "you're going to have a boring time! Why don't you buy a fishing rod?" '

Nicholas R. Winterton, MP

A secret agent from the Irish Republic was on a mission and was being parachuted behind enemy lines. When this tough little Irishman pulled the ripcord of his main parachute, after he jumped from the aircraft, nothing happened. Quickly he pulled the ripcord on his reserve parachute, but again nothing happened. 'I bet that when I get down there,' he thought to himself, 'the folding bicycle I am carrying won't work either!'

Norman Lornie
Parliamentary Affairs Officer British Airways

The flotation of British Telecom reminds me of the very first after-dinner story I ever heard, as a young newspaper reporter attending a Rotary Club dinner these many years ago in Perth. The guest speaker had been the newly appointed regional manager for the GPO telephone area and in his vote of thanks, the local Chief Constable recalled the story of the new minister in a parish asking his kirk elders if there were any folk in the parish in particular need of his prayers. Well, there was old Mrs Robertson, a martyr to arthritis. And the Widow Mackintosh with her eight bairns. And, regrettably, they had to mention Young Mary. The parish scandal was that Mary was, well, a young woman of elastic virtue whose favours were bestowed . . . but enough said. The minister was shocked, but reminded them of the desirability of loving the sinner while deploring the sin.

The very next week he met the young woman, easily recognized from their description, coming out of the village post office. Drawing a deep breath, he went up to her and said: 'My dear, I am your new minister and I have heard all about you. I just want you to know that in the few days I have been here, I have been praying regularly for you.' And she replied: 'Och, Minister, You shouldn't have bothered. I'm on the phone. . . .'

Colin Shepherd, MP

Education – or lateral thinking:

Two cannibals, father and son, in the South American jungle were inspecting their mantraps when they found in one a beautiful white girl in a state of some distress. The son, an impulsive lad, exclaimed 'Look, Dad – a white girl! Let's take her home and eat her.'

His father, who had at some time in the past acquired a certain breadth of vision from a mission school, paused thoughtfully and then said, 'No, son, let's take her home – and eat mother!'

Lord James Douglas-Hamilton, MA, LLB, MP

King Alfonso of Spain said in the Middle Ages: 'If I had been present at the creation I would have had some useful hints for the better organization of the Universe.'

Neil Thorne, OBE, TD, MP

A True Story:
My Association Chairman's wife visited her son's employer who is a Middle Eastern multimillionaire with a large family.

When greeted on arrival at his home, she was asked how many children she had.

On replying only the son who worked for him, he asked her to what she attributed her husband's lack of activity.

Michael Morris, MP

A young husband taking his wife to the maternity hospital mis-timed their departure. After a series of traffic hold-ups they arrived at the hospital just in time for her to give birth to a fine baby at the hospital entrance.

Subsequently the husband received the hospital bill to discover it included the item: delivery room, service and equipment – £30.

Most annoyed, he wrote a strong letter to the hospital administrator, pointing out that he was certainly not liable for that particular charge as his wife had been delivered of her child on the lawn outside the hospital.

Two days later he received an amended bill which included the item 'Green fee – £30'.

The Rt Hon. The Lord Chalfont, OBE, MC, PC

While I was recently in the Soviet Union I was having a drink with a Soviet general who told me that he had been informed that a university research organization in California was now using lawyers for biological experiments instead of rats. The reason, he informed me gravely, was that firstly there were more lawyers than rats in California, and secondly that there was less danger of becoming emotionally involved.

Tim Smith, MP

A story to be told with a 'wide mouth':
There was a *wide mouthed* frog. The *wide mouthed* frog went hop, hop, hop through the jungle. The *wide mouthed*

47

frog met an elephant. The elephant said 'I'm an elephant and I eat bananas and fruit and things like that.' The *wide mouthed* frog said, 'Oh, I'm a *wide mouthed* frog and I eat flies and insects and things like that.'

The *wide mouthed* frog went hop, hop, hop through the jungle. The *wide mouthed* frog met a lion. The lion said, 'I'm a lion and I eat antelope and deer and things like that.' The *wide mouthed* frog said, 'Oh, I'm a *wide mouthed* frog and I eat flies and insects and things like that.'

The *wide mouthed* frog went hop, hop, hop through the jungle. The *wide mouthed* frog met a crocodile. The crocodile said, 'I'm a crocodile and I eat *wide mouthed* frogs.' The *wide mouthed* frog said with a narrow mouth: 'Haven't seen any *wide mouthed* frogs round here.'

Norman Lornie
Parliamentary Affairs Officer British Airways

Sir David Nicolson, Chairman of Rothmans and former Chairman of British Airways, was and is a great supporter of non-executive directors in companies, saying that the breadth of outside experience they bring to the deliberations of the in-house experts provides a good balance. He tells the story of the young, newly ordained clergyman who duly prayed: 'Oh Lord, use me any way You choose in Thy service. But preferably in an advisory capacity. . . .'

The Revd W. Martin Smyth, BA, BD, MP

Marriage:

A spinster in her late thirties constantly had men friends, but when they discovered her vile temper they never proposed marriage to her. Finally, she was determined to get a particular young man, and managed to show an even temper for quite some time. Over a candlelit dinner she had specially prepared, he accidentally spilt wine over her beautiful white gown, and to his amazement she seemed unperturbed and quietly slipped upstairs to change. Convinced that the rumours were wrong, he proposed, was accepted and happily married. Soon the temper flared one night. He tackled her, saying that he had been told of her temper but had tested her out the night he had spilt the wine over her, and thought the report of her temper must have been incorrect, as she had been sweet tempered even after ruining her dress. Her reply: 'Yes, but if you had seen the mark of my teeth on the bedpost you would have known what it took to control my temper.'

The Rt Hon. David Steel, MP

When I was a young MP in the Borders, not being 100 per cent certain for how long I should address my new constituents, I asked the chairman of a local Rotary Club how long I should speak for.

In the earthy and honest manner typical of border people he replied: 'You can speak for as long as you like, laddie, but we leave here at two.'

It is sound advice that I have borne in mind ever since.

Robert Rhodes James, MP

The finest concession speech ever made:

It was made by Mo Idall who, after having been thrashed by Jimmy Carter and his Presidential hopes wrecked, merely said, 'The people have spoken – the bastards.'

Lord Redesdale

What is the difference between the European heaven and the European hell?

In the European heaven the English are the police, French the cooks, Germans the mechanics, Italians the lovers and the Swiss organize it all.

In the European hell the Germans are the police, English the cooks, French the mechanics, Swiss the lovers and the Italians organize it all.

Sir John Biggs-Davison, MP

Notice in doctor's surgery: IF YOU HAVEN'T HAD A TETANUS INJECTION IN THE LAST 5 YEARS, YOU ARE ADVISED TO SEE OUR PRACTICE NURSE.

The Rt Hon. Malcolm Rifkind, QC, MP
Secretary of State for Scotland

A number of years ago I had spoken at a public meeting in Edinburgh in favour of the need for divorce law reform and had pointed out that having been a practising advocate I was convinced that there were many people who wanted a divorce, but who, because they were not entitled to one under the strict rules then pertaining, had given perjured evidence in court for the purpose of obtaining a decree.

Shortly after a report of my comments had appeared in the newspaper, I received a telephone call from a lady in my constituency, who informed me that I was absolutely correct, as she and her husband had jointly arranged to produce false evidence in order to obtain a decree of divorce that they would not otherwise be entitled to.

For this purpose, they had arranged that a man whom the wife had never met before would be in the flat with her when a private investigator called. The wife and the man both admitted to the private investigator that they had been living together and had committed adultery. This evidence

51

was subsequently used to obtain a decree of divorce.

When the woman informed me of this over the telephone, I asked her to confirm the details in order to make sure that I had understood them correctly. I asked her if she was saying that she had been living in the flat with a man she had never met before. She confirmed that this was correct. I then asked her whether she was saying that she and this man whom she had never met before admitted committing adultery to the private investigator when he called. She confirmed that this was correct. I finally asked her to confirm that although she and this man had admitted to committing adultery in fact they never had. She replied that this also was correct. She then paused and added: 'However, I think I ought to tell you that after the private investigator left, we did!'

The Rt Hon. Donald Stewart, MP

The cannibal's wife went to the local shop to buy the Sunday lunch.

'What have you to offer me this week.'

'What about missionaries' brains?'

'We're tired of these. What else?'

'Fishermen's brains, perhaps?'

'Too salty. What else?'

'I've got politicians' brains but they're ten times as expensive as the others.'

'It's gross profiteering at that price. I'll report you to the Fair Prices Commission.'

'That would be unfair. You have no idea the number of them we have to kill to get an ounce of brains.'

Nicholas R. Winterton, MP

A new recruit, on putting to sea and suffering with sickness, said afterwards that for the first day he was afraid he would die, and for the second day he was afraid he wouldn't.

Mark Robinson, MP

A newly elected MP, quite certain that everyone in his constituency recognizes him already, is in conversation with two people at a Mayoral luncheon. During the course of the conversation he mentions the fact that he has just come back from the House of Commons, to which the person he is addressing replied, 'House of Commons? What on earth would somebody like you want to go to the House of Commons for?' 'Well,' said the MP, a bit puzzled, 'I am the Member of Parliament for this constituency.' 'Member of Parliament?' came the reply, 'I thought you were the photographer!'

Sir Kenneth Lewis, DL, MP

Harry, who had been a spiritualist, died. At a subsequent

53

circle they were able to get in touch with him. 'What's it like they asked?' 'Not too bad,' he said, 'The food is a bit dull; all salads really. But the love activity is great.' So they said, 'Splendid. You must be in Heaven.' 'Not at all: I'm a rabbit on Wimbledon Common!'

Peter Bruinvels, MP

Prayers for Parliament:
O Lord help us, we know not what we are doing.
O Lord forgive us, for all that we do do.

Alex Carlile, QC, MP

An MP and his wife were judging a beauty contest. They had to interview the three finalists. Each was asked the same question, namely, 'What would you do if you were ship-wrecked alone on a desert island, and one day woke up and found yourself surrounded by a ferocious band of angry savages, all armed to the teeth?'

The first girl, petite and demure, replied, 'I would swim away from the shore and hope to find a boat which would rescue me.'

The second girl, the practical daughter of a farmer, replied, 'I would look around to see which of the savages looked like the leader, and then I would sidle up to him and appeal engagingly for his protection.'

The MP and his wife were quite ready to give the prize to the second girl, until the third girl replied: 'I can understand the question, but what's the problem?'

The Revd W. Martin Smyth, BA, BD, MP

A young man came along to his minister to say that he wanted to get married again. The minister told him that he could only have one wife, and the man was dumbfounded. He replied that the last time he was told he could have four better, four worse, four richer, four poorer – that's sixteen. And now you tell me I can only have one.

Peter Rost, MP

My secretary – I hasten to state not the present incumbent – was intending to have some time off and in order to prepare the ground decided to write the 'thank you' letters at the same time as she accepted the invitations, and to ask a colleague to post them off at the appropriate time. All evidently went well until the Ambassador of the Federal Republic of Germany received, by the same post, my acceptance of an invitation to dinner with a glowing account of how much I had enjoyed the same occasion!

I am still reminded, from time to time, by various Germans of this *faux pas*, and I am introduced to each new

Ambassador with the words '. . . this is Peter Rost, MP. He does so enjoy our hospitality! . . .'

Sir Kenneth Lewis, DL, MP

When a man retires and time is of little importance – is it not extraordinary that they present him with a watch?

Matthew Parris, MP

I was out canvassing once when the lady I called on started to collapse and gasped out that she needed the oxygen equipment. It was too heavy to lift and so I dragged her over to it and put the mask to her mouth. When she came round her first sentiment was to gasp her thanks and her second was to say that she was a Liberal and would not be voting for me! I resisted the temptation to remove the oxygen!

Greg Knight, MP

Politicians are not the only ones who can be saved from a difficult situation by quick thinking. I rather like the story of

the young shop assistant who was working in the green grocery department when an eighteen-stone wrestler entered and asked for half a cabbage.

The young assistant went to the back of the shop and said to the manager, 'There is an idiot in the shop who wants half a cabbage.' Turning around, the assistant then suddenly noticed that the wrestler had followed him into the back of the shop. Without batting an eyelid he added, 'and this gentleman would like the other half.'

Mrs Elizabeth J. Peacock, JP, MP

I have always been of the opinion that Yorkshiremen and early Chinese philosophers had much in common – earthy clarity of thought! This is typified in the following lines from an ancient Chinese poet:

If you give a man a fish, he will have a meal.
If you teach him to fish, he will have a living.
If you are thinking a year ahead sow seed.
If you are thinking ten years ahead, plant a tree.
If you are thinking one hundred years ahead, educate the people.
By sowing seed once, you will harvest once.
By planting a tree, you will harvest tenfold.
By educating the people, you will harvest one hundred-fold.

Even for a Yorkshireman this return is acceptable. Just!

The Hon. Robert Boscawen, MC, MP

A group of British MPs visited Hong Kong. Their programme began one day by attending the early morning parade of the Royal Hong Kong Police Training College.

Drawn up in front of them were 800 magnificent young cadets, rank upon rank into the distance, bare chested in the warm conditions, ready to march off to their respective courses. Sprinkled amongst the ranks indiscriminately were those who still wore their shirts.

'Why haven't those men taken their shirts off?' asked one MP, eager to prove his keenness and attentiveness to the well-being of all present. 'Mr Jones,' growled the authoritative but quiet voice of the Commandant, 'Your Sex Discrimination Act hasn't reached us in Hong Kong yet!'

The Rt Hon. Peter walker, MBE, MP

As the twenty-two-year-old Parliamentary Candidate for Dartford in Kent I had canvassed all afternoon in a hostile area and everyone said they were voting Labour, none for me.

I knocked on a door and informed the lady I was Peter Walker, the Conservative candidate. She quickly hushed me to silence. I thought, another baby woken up, another vote lost. Then she whispered to me, 'My old man's Labour and I have told him polling day is on Friday!'

Michael Morris, MP

To be used with care:

Question to be asked early in speech and answer provided some time later.

Question: How many canaries can a Scotsman get under his kilt?

Audience encouraged to think hard about it and told the answer is quite logical.

Answer: It depends on the length of the perch.

Terence Brooks
Formerly working in Palace of Westminster

On the night that the Sexual Offences Bill got its Third Reading in the House of Lords I, as the Peers Lobby constable, thought by way of a change I'd substitute a word in the usual shout of 'House Up!' and instead shout 'Arse Up!' However, I was unfortunate in that two homosexual men were in the Peers Picture Corridor at the time, and no doubt heard what I'd shouted. One turned to me speaking in an effeminate voice and said, 'What was that you said, officer.' I, thinking quickly and to avoid any complaint said in an extremely cockney voice 'What's that, guv? Oh! we shouts it aht every night "'Ouse up".' This was pronounced so as to nearly resemble the offending word. However, the man was quicker witted than I. He said to his equally effeminate companion, 'Come along, darling. One of those ignorant Bermondsey coppers.'

Peter Bruinvels, MP

An Irish astronaut and a monkey were sent to the moon on the first-ever Irish space expedition. When the rocket landed on the moon instructions were given to both the astronaut and the monkey. The monkey's instructions were – 'Bear due east, walk 240 yards, dig $3\frac{1}{2}$ feet deep and you will find uranium.' The Irish astronaut's instructions were – 'Don't forget to feed the monkey!'

A. Cecil Walker, JP, MP

'It's rank discrimination,' complained an aging MP, 'the way the majority of me has outlived the important minority.'

The Rt Hon. J. Enoch Powell, MBE, MP

Especially after all-night sittings, I recall the story of the

Egyptian pharaoh whom an oracle warned that he had only three years to live. Determined to prove the oracle wrong, he arranged for all-night places of entertainment and spent his time moving from one to the other instead of going to bed, so that in fact he counted it as living six years before he finally succumbed. I have to admit that despite all-night sittings, I have never succeeded in getting more than seven days out of the week.

Simon Coombs, MP

A Scottish cousin of mine recently went to visit his distant relatives in Canada. They met him at the airport and took him to their imposing home in the suburbs of Vancouver.

On entering the hall of their house, he was immediately impressed by the wide array of antlered heads on the walls. One in particular, a many-antlered beast, stared down at him haughtily from the end wall.

'Och, ma God,' he said in his quaint Scottish way, 'what's thaaat?'

'Why,' replied his Canadian cousin, 'but that's a moose.'

'Och, but if thaaat's a moose, what are the caaats like?!'

Steve Norris, MP

A chap from our village got engaged and when he told his

father the good news, was horrified to hear his father say, 'I'm awfully sorry, Son. I should have told you about some of my little fun and games when I was a lad. I'm afraid you can't marry young Mary – you see, she's a relation.'

The poor chap was shattered but a couple of years later was able to impart similar news to his father. The response was crushing. 'I suppose I really should have made a clean breast of all of this but I'm afraid you can't marry her either, you see I really did have a good time when I was young and she's a relation too.'

Our boy was devastated and when his mother found him moping amd miserable, he poured his heart out to her and told her the whole story. 'Oh don't worry about that,' said his mother, 'Your father's no relation of yours anyway.'

Michael Meadowcroft, MP

Last June, as I drove into Leeds, it was clear that the flash floods had caused a lot of damage. As I opened the front door I could hear the telephone ringing. Could I please come round straightaway, help was urgently needed.

The flood water had gone straight through the house, rising above living room window level, carrying away greenhouses and knocking doors off hinges.

My constituent stood outside describing what had happened. 'The water came down that hill, opposite,' she said, 'and it wasn't just rain water – it was full of affluence and increment.'

It's not often you get a double!

The Rt Hon. John Wakeham, MP
Government Chief Whip

A pessimist is one who takes prunes with his All-Bran.

Richard Needham, MP

New Minister visiting hospital in Northern Ireland for the first time. Surrounded by consultants, administrators, nurses and civil servants. Ushered into mother just commenced her labour.

'How are you?' says the Minister jovially.

Groans.

'Oh, is this your first time?'

'No it is my twelfth.'

'We've had Mrs O'Hara here every year,' chips in the Sister.

'Does her husband come along?'

'No.'

'Perhaps he's in the pub.'

'He doesn't drink.'

Exasperated Minister.

'But don't worry, my dear, there will be lots of lovely healthy screams.'

'I'm not intending to scream.'

David Amess, MP

Whilst on a Standing Committee discussing what proved to be a contentious Bill, the Opposition Member with great humour was engaged in a filibuster. I seem to remember his speaking for at least five hours continuously during a night sitting. Before not too long various members of the Committee became distracted or even 'dozed off'. The Chairman of the Committee not only fell into a deep sleep but began to snore quite loudly throughout the proceedings. I should hasten to add that no one attempted to wake him up and I was probably the only one listening, and began to get an embarrassing attack of the giggles at the bizarre situation I found myself in. At the end of the Hon. Member's filibuster a Division was called and the loud voice of the attendant calling Division, combined with a nudge in the ribs, woke the Chairman. He looked about the room as everyone began to smile and said, 'You need not worry, I know I have not missed anything. The Committee has been on automatic pilot!'

Sydney Bidwell, MP

Some years ago a granddaughter, child of my daughter, was told that I would be on television commenting on out-standing news items following the ITV post one o'clock news. Robert Kee was the questioner. I remember it well because Ronald Reagan, aspiring then as US President, was on the programme too when making a visit to London.

I later asked my young granddaughter what she thought of the programme. She replied, 'Why did that man (Mr Kee) call you Mr Bidwell?' 'But that is my name,' I said. 'Is it then,' said she. 'Why not Grandad?'

Norman Lornie
Parliamentary Affairs Officer British Airways

In the days before the Licensing (Scotland) Act of 1960, which regularized pub closing times among other things, that sad refrain 'Last Orders Please' occurred at widely differing times from one part of the country to the other. Willie Merrilees, late Chief Constable of the Lothian counties around Edinburgh, was a great fisherman and used to tell of a holiday visit to a small hotel in the extreme northwest of Scotland. As a resident, he could drink in the lounge all day and all night, but he noticed after a few days that the bar itself was still a hive of activity well into the night, with locals dropping in without let or hindrance. Purely in a spirit of enquiry, he happened to ask the landlord: 'What time do you usually close up here?' To which mine host replied: 'Weel, Sir, it depends on the fishin', but usually towards the end of October.'

Greg Knight, MP

A worried young man attends the advice surgery of his MP: 'I am very worried. I have married three women without getting a divorce. Can I be charged with bigotry?'

MP: 'No, No, No. You have got it all wrong. If you have married three women that is not bigotry. Its trigonometry.'

Barry Sheerman, MP

Two Members on the left of the Party observed Herbert Morrison walking through the park to Speaker's Corner every Saturday morning with a copy of *Marxism Today* (or whatever the current publication was). One said to the other, 'I don't know if you can absorb Marxism through the armpit, but I've never seen the bugger open it.'

Simon C. Barnes
Secretary Bristol West Young Conservatives

Prime Ministers hate nothing more than continuous bad publicity, and it is the job of a good Press Officer to make sure that it ends quickly. Once, in the (bad old) days of

Harold Wilson's premiership, a scandal was persistently getting headline news coverage. Wilson decided to take a break from it all and went to his beloved Scilly Isles for a week's holiday. Fortunately, while he was away, a foul murder occurred in London which filled all the newspapers and TV news, sending other items to the back pages. When he returned, Wilson summoned his Press Officer, exclaiming that he knew his Press Officer was efficient, but he didn't expect him to go THAT FAR.

Greg Knight, MP

A middle-aged MP visits his doctor because he is having problems with sexual matters.

'What is wrong with your sex life?' enquires the GP.

'Infrequent!' responded the MP.

The doctor looked at him. 'Is that one word or two,' he asked.

Mrs Edwina Currie, MP

Children are often a 'chip off the old block'. But faced with the evidence from one's own children, one sometimes wonders. . . .

Susie was barely two and a half when our house in Birmingham was used in a by-election as main headquarters following the death of a leading local councillor. For weeks it was like living in a railway station. But the tot loved it – greeting everyone at the door, showing them where to sign in and collect their leaflets, then firmly shoving them back out into the cold to get going.

The night before the by-election, I wearily fed the children their tea, and said, 'It will all be over soon and then we can have our house back, won't that be nice?' But Susie pulled a face. 'What's the matter?' I asked her. 'Well, Mummy,' she said, explaining it all carefully to me, 'Nice ladies and gentlemen come. And they give me sweeties. And they say, "Don't you tell your Mummy!" '

And sure enough, a search of her room found a drawer full of chocolate bars. Am I really like that?

Sir Kenneth Lewis, DL, MP

An Irishman who wanted a house thought he was bound to get one when he went into the British Home Stores.

Greg Knight, MP

I like the story of the young punk rocker who went to see his MP.

The young man, clad in leather and chains, was annoyed that the police had charged him with speeding on the motorway. 'It's unfair victimization,' he protested.

The MP started to take details of the case with the intention of complaining to the Chief Constable about the matter. However, he was surprised when the young lad admitted that he had been travelling at over 90 mph.

'Why do you object to being summonsed when you are obviously guilty of the offence?' his MP enquired.

'Because my driving licence permits me to speed,' the punk replied.

Incredulous, the MP asked to see the document, which appeared to be a standard driving licence.

'Where does this licence say that you can speed?' the MP demanded.

'Here,' replied the punk, 'where it says "tear along the dotted line".'

Peter Bruinvels, MP

The Times' political correspondent has just done his annual survey on who the 1983 intake of Members of Parliament would like to be leader, if Mrs Thatcher was run over by a bus.

My answers were:
1. The Bus driver wouldn't dare to run the PM over.
2. If Mrs Thatcher was run over, she would just get up and continue to lead our country, as before!

Geoff Lawler, MP

Following a visit to my surgery I agreed to visit a constituent's home to see at first hand evidence of rats in his cellar.

We sat down opposite a wall and waited five minutes when suddenly a fish jumped out of the crack. I turned to my constituent and said, 'Did you see that, a great big fish just jumped out of the floor?' He replied, 'Never mind the damp, its the rats you've come to look at.'

Ron Brown, MP

When I first came to London as an MP, I used to stay in a small hotel in Pimlico run by a Scot. He could never understand my strange hours, let alone the large briefcase with piles of bumf sticking out of every corner.

Every morning, polite as ever, he would enter into conversation about my occupation, but deftly I managed to parry his questions.

One morning, however, he became exasperated, asking right out: 'So what do you do then?'

'Oh, I'm an engineer,' I said with some truth, but really not wishing to get into a harangue about politics over my porridge.

'That's a relief,' he gasped, 'I thought you were a VAT man!'

The Rt Hon. Donald Stewart, MP

The village blacksmith disappeared from a Scottish village. No trace of him could be found.

Years later, a former school chum of his walked into a chemist's shop in the English Midlands and recognized the former blacksmith.

'What are you doing passing yourself off as a chemist. You've had no training. You'll poison half the population of England.'

'Ach,' said the 'chemist' shrugging his shoulders, 'It'll take a hell of a long time to make up for Flodden.'

Geoff Lawler, MP

A Socialist MP was addressing a meeting and getting animated feedback from the audience: 'What about the Tories?' cried one . . . 'Drive them underground,' said the MP.

'What about the capitalists?' said another. Back came the response, 'Drive them underground.'

'What about the prostitutes?' shouted one. 'Drive them underground' was the response.

One chap turns to another at the back, 'Typical, pampering the flippin' miners again.'

Jim Graigen, MLitt, FBIM, JP, MP

'Is he someone you could accompany on a tiger hunt?' I asked. 'Well, let's just say,' came the reply, 'you would be safer with the tiger!'

Sir John Biggs-Davison, MP

Vicar on his parish rounds calls on a lady living alone. She replies to his knock: 'Is that you, angel?'
Vicar: 'No, but I'm from the same department.'

David Amess, MP

How obvious remarks can backfire:
  After attending an important service at a church in my constituency I was introduced to various 'worthies' outside the church, and in particular to one gentleman who proudly introduced me to his mother who was ninety-eight. I was left with her for a little while and to make conversation said that I very much looked forward to attending her 100th birthday party celebrations in a couple of years' time. She sternly looked me in the eye and said, 'What a dreadful thing to wish anyone to live to be 100.' Oh dear!

Ivan Lawrence, QC, MP

George of Denmark asked Charles the Second what to do to lose weight. King Charles replied, 'Walk with me; hunt with my brother; and look to your wife.'

Sir Kenneth Lewis, DL, MP

Two Irishmen in a car – the passenger carrying a big parcel on his lap.

Said to his mate, the driver, who was going rather fast on a bumpy road – 'For goodness sake, go easy Paddy. You know perfectly well I've got a bomb on my lap!'

'Not to worry,' said Paddy to the driver, 'there's another one in the boot!'

Michael Colvin, MP

The Ministry of Defence memorandum which arrived on the Officer's desk was not to his liking.

'Balls', he wrote in large letters and ticked his name on the distribution list.

As he threw it into the 'Out' tray he noticed that the next

addressee was a member of the Women's Royal Army Corps. He grabbed the memorandum, deleted 'balls' and wrote on instead 'round objects'.

A week later the memorandum came back to him from the General Officer Commanding with a curt note attached asking, 'Who is Mr Round, and what does he object to?'!

Norman Lornie
Parliamentary Affairs Officer British Airways

Sir Edward Appleton, as Principal and Vice-Chancellor of Edinburgh University, used to tell of his own first-ever visit to Edinburgh. Sir Edward, who had been a government scientist, came up from London to attend an international scientific convention in Edinburgh just after the end of World War Two and, as he said, he and virtually all the delegates were dressed in the standard uniform of dark overcoat and black homburg hat. At the end of the first day's session, he went down to the cloakroom of the North British Hotel. Even as he approached the cloakroom attendant across the great width of the marble floor, the old chap turned and retrieved a hat and coat, and it was already lying across the counter for him before he produced his cloakroom ticket. Sir Edward duly noted that it was indeed his property and expressed some astonishment, never having set foot in the place before. 'How on earth did you know that was my hat and coat?' he asked. And the old attendant looked at him balefully and replied: 'I dinna know it's yours, Sir; all I know is this – it's the one you gave me when you came in.'

Greg Knight, MP

The following exchange is reported to have taken place in a House of Commons corridor.

Backbench MP (to Government Minister): 'Do you believe in free speech?'

Minister: 'Why, of course.'

Backbench MP: 'Good. Can you make one in my constituency next week?'

David Heathcoat-Amory, FCA, MP

My uncle, Derick Heathcoat-Amory, was campaigning in the Tiverton constituency during the 1945 General Election. He was well known locally, but mainly as a sporting man having been a Master of the Tiverton Foxhounds before the war.

At a meeting in one of the more remote villages Derick spoke for about half an hour on the great issues of the day. When he finished the Chairman asked for questions. There was a long silence with some shifting of chairs and muffled coughs. In desperation the Chairman said: 'Surely there must be someone with a question for our candidate. This election will decide the future of our country.' Eventually an old man at the back of the hall put up his hand: 'When are you going to bring the hounds here again, Mr Derick?'

Whatever answer my uncle was able to give, he won the election comfortably.

Simon C. Barnes
Secretary Bristol West Young Conservatives

All politicians believe that the Press treats them unfairly and with total bias. One MP was getting very irritated by a lobby correspondent from the *Evening Gazette* when the reporter said, 'We are only seeking the truth.' The MP turned to him and shouted: 'Throughout history man has been seeking the truth, and you tell me that the *Gazette* prints it every Monday night!'

The Hon. Greville Janner, QC, MP

Division Bell:
  Two American tourists were in the Central Lobby when the Division Bell rang. 'I wonder what that means?' said one.
  'I don't know,' replied the other. 'But I expect that one of them must have escaped!'

The Rt Hon. Patrick Jenkin, MP

'My professionals':

After the Seven-Day War in the Egyptian desert, the victorious Moshe Dayan was interviewed by the Press.

'To what do you ascribe your great victory, General?' they asked.

'To my professionals,' he replied.

'You mean professional soldiers?' they asked.

'No, no,' he answered: 'my brigade of the professions – solicitors, accountants, estate agents, architects, actuaries and above all the barristers!'

'Why, what's so marvellous about them?'

'When I stand up in my tank and shout "Charge", God, how they charge!'

John Hannam, MP

A man was on holiday in the South of France in lovely weather and received a telegram stating:

'Mother-in-law dead. Shall we embalm, bury or cremate?'

He sent a cable back stating:

'Take no chances – do all three.'

Geoffrey Dickens, JP, MP

When canvassing at election time I called on an attractive young lady who said she would vote for me if I got her council flat put in her name. She told me that after seven days of marriage she thought that her husband was a sex maniac. This young beauty then insisted on giving me an example, despite my protests. 'There I was, just standing there looking at all the chickens when he leapt on top of me to have his way.' 'Good gracious,' I said, 'but you know that's fairly normal after only seven days.' She said, 'What, in Sainsbury's?'

Lord Hill of Luton

In Brighton she was Brenda
She was Patsy up in Perth
In Cambridge she's Clarissa
The sweetest thing on earth
In Stafford she is Stella
The pick of all the bunch
But down on his expense account
She's Petrol, Oil and Lunch.

Sir Geoffrey Johnson Smith, MP

At the time I made this statement I was in my waders attempting to land a large rainbow trout in the company of some Labour MPs during the annual charity fishing match when a team from the House of Commons challenge a team from the Salmon and Trout Association.

I had carefully attached a 'leader' to my line and it was then promptly hooked by an overweight trout, which had me running up and down the bank as I tried to land it – crying (to the astonishment of those present) – 'I have no faith in my leader.'

The Revd W. Martin Smyth, BA, BD, MP

Today's economic situation:
Agent to Tenant: 'I called today to tell you that we are raising your rent.'
Tenant: 'That's good, for I can't raise it myself.'

Alfred Dubs, MP

Just after first being elected, I was due to take part in a

Consolidated Fund debate, something that goes on all night. My newness to the job made me feel a little silly walking into the House of Commons at about midnight. Also I had all the pomposity of a newly elected MP, which I hope I have now lost. The policewoman at the door said, 'Good evening, Sir.' Feeling I had to justify myself I said, 'Good evening, I am hoping to speak tonight.' The policewoman replied, 'Yes Sir, will it make any difference?' She was right. I was called to speak at 5.30 am, the Press Gallery was empty and only a few colleagues waiting to speak, the Deputy Speaker, the Minister and an official and the Hansard reporters were there. It made no difference.

Robin Corbett, MP

A friend happens to work for Mr Robert Maxwell, the ebullient proprietor of Mirror Group Newspapers. Ever since he bought the business, my friend has had the same questions asked by acquaintances every time they spot him. 'What is he like?'

This friend happened to be at a rather grand function and he was introduced to the Prince of Wales who, as soon as he heard my friend's job, came out with the question: 'What is he like?'

A few minutes later, Princess Alexandra and her husband were introduced to him . . . and exactly the same sequence of events took place. My friend is now considering having a card printed with the answer to that question and naturally, he hopes to include the 'By Royal Appointment' warrant.

Richard Holt, MP

Two police outriders were motorcycling along in front of the judge's car on the way to the Crown Court Assizes. Two further policemen on motor cycles brought up the rear. Passing through the main street a resident was clearly seen to make a Harvey Smith gesture at the cavalcade, where upon one of the police outriders seized upon and arrested the man in question, who was an hour later hauled up in front of the judge on a charge of contempt. Asked by the judge to explain his action, the man said, 'It's all a case of mistaken identity, Sir.' To which the policeman said, 'No, it's not, it was you.' 'Ah,' said the man, 'my mistaken identity – as you went past I thought it was the Town Mayor.' The judge dismissed the case and awarded the man £5 out of public funds.

Lord Hooson, QC

What about the Nye Bevan story when a rather ancient and decrepit Tory MP got up to attack the National Health Bill when it was going through the House and Bevan was heard to observe, 'Strange that they should have sent such a frail vehicle to carry such a load of nonsense.'

Lord James Douglas-Hamilton, MA, LLB, MP

One of the relatives of an old Scotsman called Hamish called at the lawyers of Hamish, having heard that Hamish was no longer alive, to ask whether before departing he left a deed. He had heard a rumour that Hamish had left £30,000.

To his dismay the lawyer replied, 'No, he did not leave £30,000,' and then after a long pause he added, 'Hamish has been taken away for it.'

Jerry Hayes, MP

I remember when I was first called to the Bar, sitting behind an eminent QC – it was rather an unpleasant case where a young woman was alleging that his client had indecently assaulted her. The case had been going very badly and I wondered what, if anything could be done to save the miserable skin of the defendant. At last the time came for the eminent barrister to cross-examine the poor unfortunate victim. 'Madam,' he said, 'it is right is it not that you say that my client had attacked you in the most disgusting way?' 'Yes,' she immediately replied. 'Madam, is it not also right that after this intimacy had taken place, you fled from your flat, naked?' 'Yes,' she replied. 'And furthermore, is it not right that your naked body was clothed with the doormat?' 'Yes,' she replied, somewhat puzzled. 'But,'

87

roared the eminent Counsel, 'is it not the fact that on this doormat was the word – WELCOME?'

Hugh Dykes, MP

An MP is overworked and exhausted at endless surgeries and an endless queue of insoluble problems. Finally his mind flips and one late night after a long surgery, he suffers a complete breakdown and loss of identity.

Speaking feverishly across the desk to a 'patient' who is obviously mad too, he says: 'Well, your problem is a tough one, so, if I were you . . . pause . . . which I am. . . .!'

Michael Howard, QC, MP

When a judge asks a barrister a question to which the barrister does not know the answer, the barrister will frequently ask for permission to 'take instructions' from his solicitor in the hope that inspiration may become available.

On one famous occasion a judge was getting increasingly irritated by the arguments being addressed to him by the barrister in the case. At last he could contain himself no longer. 'What do you take me for, Mr Jones,' asked the judge, 'some kind of chump?' 'Would your lordship permit me to take instructions?' asked the barrister.

A. Cecil Walker, JP, MP

'What is the definition of Irish foreplay?'
'Brace yourself – Bridget.'

Gerald Howarth, MP

Shortly after being elected to Parliament in 1983 I received a congratulatory note from my Scottish godfather and uncle. It was written on a postcard and contained the following brief but pointed message:

'Congratulations! Politicians are like bananas; they arrive green, turn yellow and are invariably bent. But I hope you will do better.'

Philip Hunter

A sultan, who lived in a remote village in the Sahara, was a table tennis fanatic. His only daughter had two eminent suitors apply for her hand. He called the suitors to him, told them to go out into the world, and that the one returning with the most ping-pong balls would have the right to marry his daughter.

Six months later the first suitor returned with a camel-train full of ping-pong balls. The Sultan exclaimed with delight and a date for the marriage was set. Some weeks later the sultan was called to the edge of the village, it was the custom for him to greet travellers. A bloody wreck of a man with only one eye, one arm and one leg was dragging a bloody sack behind him as he crawled toward the village. The sultan had just arranged for transport to the new hospital when he recognized the other suitor. 'But you can't have many ping-pong balls in that sack?' he queried. 'Oh no,' came the reply, 'I thought you said King Kong balls!'

The Rt Hon. Sir Edward du Cann, KBE, MP

Each day, before the House of Commons begins its work, prayers are said by the Speaker.

'Considering the state of the nation,' observed one cynic, 'it would seem that Members' prayers are pretty ineffective.'

'Reflect how much worse affairs might be,' replied the MP, 'if no prayers at all were said.'

When there is in power a government whose legislative proposals I do not approve of, I have a solemn little prayer of my own. It runs thus:

'God bless this assembly, and may He overrule its deliberations to the benefit of the common people.'

At times we may all say Amen to that.

Gerald Howarth, MP

In my earlier banking days in the City I worked under a Scottish Managing Director who was extremely well travelled and could claim an impressive list of contacts in all walks of life around the world.

Knowing how useful a little French or German can be in developing business in foreign parts, I asked him how he had managed to get by with the scantiest knowledge of any foreign language. He responded by saying, 'It's quite easy really. There's only two things you need to know in a foreign language. The first is "Which way is the gentleman's?", the second "My friend will pay." '

Clement Freud, MP

A golfer went to the professional's shop, paid for a round of golf and asked whether he might hire a caddy. He explained that he hit the ball pretty hard, kept his eye on the ball the way it said one should in the golf manuals . . . and therefore needed someone with a sharp eye to follow the line of his shots.

They produced a caddy; the golfer looked at him and said, 'How old are you?'

'Eighty-three,' said the caddy.

'Listen,' said the golfer, 'I hit the ball very hard; keep my head down like it says I should, and need someone with perfect vision.'

'I have twenty-twenty vision,' said the old caddy.

They went to the first tee and the golfer hit the ball very hard, keeping his head down.

'Did you see where it went?' he asked the caddy.

'Yes, Sir.'

'Where?'

'I've forgotten.'

Derek Conway, MP

Told to me on a visit to some troops on exercise:
'How can you tell when a politician is lying – his lips move.'

Simon C. Barnes
Secretary Bristol West Young Conservatives

When canvassing recently in Bristol, I called at a house where a charming old lady answered the door. On asking if I could speak to her husband, she replied that he had passed away the week before. I humbly apologized and offered my sympathy, but she suddenly said: 'Oh you needn't worry – he's sent in a postal vote for you.'

David Mitchell, MP

In the autumn of 1985 Ministers in the Department of Transport had to assess the relative merits of the following propositions for a cross-channel link – bridge, tunnel, Euro-route or Jones Brothers of Somerset.

The first three were multi-million-pound projects – Jones Brothers £30,000. David Mitchell questioned Mr Jones, one of the directors, who explained that he was going to start digging at Dover and his brother at Calais and they hoped to meet in the middle.

'But what,' said a perplexed Transport Minister, 'if you don't meet at the same place in the middle?'

'Ah,' said Mr Jones, with that attractive Somerset burr. 'Then we'll keep on digging and you will get two tunnels for the price of one. You support small businesses, don't you?'

John Cope, MP
Government Deputy Chief Whip

Three days after Sir Ronald Storrs became the first Christian Governor of Jerusalem since the Crusades in 1918, he received the following letter from an Arab seeking a boon, and trying to adapt his style to the new circumstances: 'I beseech your excellency to grant my request, for the sake of J. Christ, Esq, a gentleman whom your honour closely resembles.'

Terence Brooks
Formerly working in Palace of Westminster

A gentlemanly Conservative MP was in the Post Office situated in the Members Lobby, enquiring as to whether Sir John Barlow was a Baronet. He said to the postman, 'I say, is Sir John Barlow a Bart?' 'I dunno guv, I ain't seen,' came the cockney reply.

Patrick Cormack, FSA, MP

A vicar in my constituency was entertaining the bishop and his wife for dinner. Just before they were due to go in for the meal a tiny head appeared around the door and the flustered parents realized that the children had not gone to sleep after all.

'Never mind, my dear,' said the bishop patting the head of six-year-old Jennifer. 'You shall say grace.' To which a confused child said to a despairing mother, 'Mummy, what is grace.'

As the father saw his thoughts of preferment going out of the window mother said, 'You know, dear, its what I said before breakfast this morning.'

At which Jennifer putting her hands together said, 'Oh God why did I ask this man to dinner!'

George Robertson, MP

The Red Army Captain is having his hair cut. 'And how was Afganistan?' asked the barber. 'Dull and routine,' replies the Captain. 'But surely something is going on in Afganistan,' persists the barber. 'No nothing,' responds the Captain. 'But it must be exciting in Afganistan?' tries the barber again. 'Just why are you so curious about Afganistan,' says the Captain. 'I'm not curious at all,' comes back the barber, 'But any time I mention Afganistan your hair stands on end and its much easier to cut!'

John Corrie, MP

The pilot on the shuttle up to Glasgow came on and did the usual bit about flying at 33,000 feet, at 530 mph over the ground and all was clear for our landing at Glasgow and wished us a pleasant flight. He forgot to switch off the intercom and his co-pilot asked him what he was going to do in Glasgow. 'I'm going to have a hot bath, a large drink and then make love to that beautiful blond hostess we have on board.'

The poor hostess in utter embarrassment rushed down the plane and tripped and fell. An old lady looked down with a deep frown and said, 'It's all right, lassie, there's no hurry – he's having a drink and a bath first!'

Earl Amherst, MC

During a tour of South Africa, the former President of the United States, Richard M. Nixon, while stopping off in Ghana was said to have asked a distinguished-looking young Negro, 'Now that you have got rid of those God-damned British, how do you feel about your new freedom?' to which the young man replied, 'I'se knows nothing about freedom, Boss, I'se from Alabama.'

Jim Craigen, MLitt, FBIM, JP, MP

The Glasgow Bailie is reputed to have told the accused, 'Thirty days without the option of a fine. And count yourself lucky. If there had been a shred of evidence against you it would have been ninety!'

Mrs Edwina Currie, MP

The Derbyshire air produces longevity and wit. They seem to like their MPs 'interesting' rather than identikit, thank goodness, but there's no doubt we are put firmly in our place at times.

Recently I was asked to a 100th birthday celebration for Molly, a lady in a residential home in the constituency. 'Do come,' said the matron, 'she takes a great interest in you. There will be a glass of sherry at 11.00 am.'

By the time I got there, the birthday girl and the other residents had already been at the sherry awhile and she was holding forth, saying how old age brought a diminution of the senses – 'You can't see, you can't 'ear, it's 'orrible.' So I graciously gave her a box of House of Commons mints and wishing her many happy returns, waited for an appropriate response. None came; she peered at me with a rheumy eye and carried on chatting.

My vanity surfaced. 'Do you know who I am?' I asked helpfully. 'Oh yes, ducky,' she replied dismissively and turned again to her neighbour. 'Well, tell me then: who am I?' I asked. Irritated, she reached for the sherry and announced, 'You? Oh yes. You're that piece on the telly, aren't you?'

The matron got very flustered and apologetic. As she showed me out, she whispered that Molly always got it wrong particularly after a nip or two; she had meant to say, 'You're my MP and I've seen you on the telly.' But I prefer the clear testimony of at least one constituent that all those taxis at 5.30 am for breakfast TV are having some effect!

Lord James Douglas-Hamilton, MA, LLB, MP

On addressing the Argyle and Sutherland Highlanders during the Second World War, Sir Winston Churchill looked at them with a fierce expression saying, 'There is only one thing wrong with you. There are not enough of you.'

A. Cecil Walker, JP, MP

Two pretty students had returned from a late date and were getting ready for bed. 'My date was so persistent,' one of the girls said. 'Why he should know that there are some things a girl should not do before eighteen!'

'You're so right, honey' said the other. 'I wouldn't enjoy a big audience either!'

Nicholas Baker, MP

The vicar called on one of his parishioners who had recently moved into a house in the parish. Looking round the garden, the vicar beamed. 'You and God have done very good work in the garden.' Came the reply, 'I have been living here for six months and the garden was in a terrible state when God had it all to himself.'

Simon C. Barnes
Secretary Bristol West Young Conservatives

I am often asked as a Conservative, what the difference is between the Monday Club and the Tory Reform Group. I have found it easiest to answer that they are both much the same: Monday Clubbers believe Mrs Thatcher is the best ever leader of the Party, Tory Reform Group members agree – she is the best ever leader . . . since Edward Heath.

Ian Mikardo, MP

Last year contractors carrying out large-scale building operations in London were warned against a well-dressed man who was turning up at work sites claiming to be a building inspector and then planting a bomb at some vulnerable point on the site.

One day a well-dressed man turned up at a work-site in East London and told the site foreman that he was a building inspector and wanted to have a look round.

The site foreman was highly sceptical. 'You are not a building inspector,' he said; 'you know nothing whatever about building.'

'Oh yes I do,' said the visitor, 'I am an expert.'

The foreman snorted. 'Expert my foot – you would not know the difference between a girder and a joist.'

'Oh yes I do,' said the visitor. 'Girder wrote *Faust*, and Joist wrote *Ulysses*.'

101

Ivan Lawrence, QC, MP

I recently asked a visiting Prime Minister what he thought of his meeting with Mrs Thatcher. He replied, 'I had heard that she was the Iron Lady. I did not feel any of the iron, but I felt a lot of the lady.'

Mrs Edwina Currie, MP

Debbie was older – ten or so – when she became a weekly boarder at a local school. On Sunday evenings I sent her off with a pile of fruit, to encourage sensible eating habits. Back came a message one week in summer asking me to desist: biscuits and sweets were acceptable but not fruit.

Highly indignant, I fired off a letter asking why not. And a rather grubby note was put into my hand by said child at the end of the week, from her housemistress.

'It's not that I object to fruit as such; but I do object to Debbie stuffing rotten peaches down the beds of the other girls.'

Oh dear. Debbie was duly summoned, face solemn but eyes dancing.

'Did you put a rotten peach in somebody's bed?'

'No, Mummy.'

'But it says here that you did.'

'Well, it wasn't rotten when I put it there. . . .'

David Mudd, MP

A Cornish jeweller whose ingenuity exceeded his scruples bought several thousand pounds' worth of gems on credit. He put them into a coffin, rented a hearse and headed for England with his loot.

On the Devon end of the Tamar Bridge a customs man stopped him and asked what the hearse was doing.

'Can't you see?', asked the jeweller. 'It's a funeral.'

'It's a strange funeral that has no mourners,' said the official. 'Where are they?'

'I'll tell you,' said the jeweller. 'They're coming along behind. Some will turn up in thirty days, some will be here in sixty days, and the rest will come along in ninety days.'

Sir John Biggs-Davison, MP

A severe Irish judge sentenced a frail old reprobate to twenty years. There were tears in court when the accused exclaimed: 'I'm a very old man, my lord; I'll never do that sentence.' The judge: 'Well, try to do as much of it as you can.'

Another prisoner before him complained that he had not had a fair crack of the whip; so the judge added twenty strokes of the cat to the sentence.

Sydney Bidwell, MP

Just after my election to Parliament for the first time in 1966, local Indian people asked the Indian Government to invite me to visit their country. I was offered full co-operation. After a long flight accompanied by my wife, we were received by a welcoming party at Bombay Airport. The charming leader outlined a busy several days of visits. Unfortunately, I was suffering from a raging, agonizing toothache. I explained.

They took us off to Bombay dental hospital, where the offending molar was extracted by a turbanned expert (making me feel at home). Soon the hospital principal, a jolly man, came to see how I was faring. I was OK, greatly relieved and out of pain. The head man said, 'When we heard a British MP was coming to us, we were a little concerned but when we realized he was in pain, we knew he was likely to have his mouth shut!'

The Rt Hon. Lord Boyd-Carpenter, DL

The late Mr Justice McCardie, whose judgements had recently suffered a good deal at the hands of the Court of Appeal, was trying a case in which the sobriety of one of the parties was in issue.

A witness had said, 'I would not say he was as sober as a judge and I would not say he was as drunk as a lord.'

'You mean,' said Mr Justice McCardie, 'that he was in that intermediate condition which one associates with a Lord Justice of Appeal?'

Stephen Ross, MP

Like many colleagues I make numerous Christmas visits to old people's homes and hospitals. Arriving late at one such establishment I was met by the Mayor and Mayoress who were obviously itching to have their tea, kindly provided by the management. I therefore hurriedly shook hands and exchanged niceties with the fifty elderly ladies and the one man (such is the ratio by which they outlive us) when I came up to the fifty-second resident. I breezily enquired if she would be having visitors to see her on Christmas Day, to which came the somewhat frozen response. 'Don't you recognize me?' 'Afraid I don't,' said I. 'I'm the Lady Mayoress, you fool!'

I don't think they voted for me at the last election!

The Revd W. Martin Smyth, BA, BD, MP

Denominations in religion:

There are so many sects that they prey on one another rather than pray for one another.

Lord Airedale

In a city centre in the Sudan there stands – or stood – a remarkable statue of General Gordon astride a camel.

A British administrator, on being posted elsewhere, asked his small son what he would like to do on his last day.

The boy opted for a last look at Gordon's statue.

His father, much gratified by a desire so noble in one so young, readily granted the request.

Together they stood before the statue in silence. They walked round it. As they turned to leave the scene the boy said, 'Daddy, who is that man who sits on Gordon?'

Peter Bruinvels, MP

Sign seen in the back of a car during a recent by-election: Make your MP work – don't re-elect him!

Nicholas Baker, MP

The meaning of ethics:

When someone comes into the shop, offers a pound note for which you give change, goes away and then you realize that he has given a five-pound note. Ethics means whether or not you tell your partner.

Earl Amherst, MC

In a crowded court room a coloured lady, a Mrs Jones, was trying to help her daughter in an action for rape. 'But,' said the judge, 'from the records it seems this is by no means the first time such a thing has happened to your daughter. How do you account for that?' 'Yas, Sir, Yas, Sir, Yer Honour, But she do seem to rape so awful easy.'

Ivan Lawrence, QC, MP

Chicken to mother hen. 'Mummy, Mummy, am I people?'
'No, darling, you're chicken.'
'Mummy, Mummy, was I born?'
'No, darling, you were laid.'
'Mummy, Mummy, are people laid?'
'Well, darling, some are and some are chicken.'

Earl Amherst, MC

It was a few days before Christmas at a street corner in Soho, a Greek was chatting to a Chinaman, mostly about nothing. The Greek started chiding the Chinaman about his inability to pronounce the letter 'R'. 'Melly Chlistmas, indeed. What is this rubbish?' A year later, almost to the day and at the same street corner there they were again. The Chinaman went up to the Greek and with a hint of triumph in his voice and stressing the 'Rs' wished him a 'Very, Very Merry Christmas, you Gleek Plick.'

Norman Lornie
Parliamentary Affairs Officer British Airways

The great Professor Donald Francis Tovey of Edinburgh used to delight in a story that long pre-dated the National Health Service. In the 1930s he often told the tale of the old Scottish minister who regularly thundered against his flock that they would be sure to end up towards the bottom of the bottomless pit, weepin' an' wailin' an' gnashing their teeth. And looking round his predominently elderly congregation, would add: '. . . and for those of you who nae longer have any teeth, teeth will be provided.'

Sir John Biggs-Davison, MP

When I was first adopted as Parliamentary Candidate in Essex, I became political inheritor, as a result of the redistribution of constituencies, of many former electors of Sir Winston Churchill.

Naturally, we invited the great but ageing statesman to speak for me. We took our biggest hall. The international, national and local Press were fully represented. Sir Winston delivered a magnificent speech on world affairs. My supporters were eager, however, for some words of commendation and encouragement for their new, young candidate – me. Eventually, Sir Winston came down to Essex earth. He half turned round on the platform and pointed at me. 'Ladies and Gentlemen,' he growled, 'you have a fine candidate here – in Clark.'

Clark was the name of my Labour opponent.

Cranley Onslow, MP

An English visitor to the USA, in New York for the first time, was strongly advised by American friends that it was very unwise to go for a walk alone, in the dusk, in Central Park. The chance of being mugged, he was told, was very high.

So, of course, he went for a walk in Central Park at dusk, and alone, that very evening. It was perfectly peaceful: there seemed to be no one else about. Then, suddenly, a little man dashed round a corner, bumped heavily into him, and scuttled away.

The Englishman, startled, felt in his pocket, and found his wallet wasn't there. Furious, he turned and ran after the little man, overtook him, and seized him by the collar. 'Give me that wallet,' he shouted.

The little man dropped a wallet on the ground, wriggled free and dashed away again. The Englishman picked the wallet up, congratulated himself on recovering it so easily, and walked quietly back to his hotel. There he went up to his room, let himself in with his key, and saw his own wallet lying on the bed where he had left it.

John Townend, FCA, MP

Grace:
   Give us the strength and power to eat this lot in half-an-hour.

Christopher Patten, MP

You may recall that in the notorious trial of D. H. Lawrence's *Lady Chatterley's Lover*, the Prosecuting Counsel concluded his remarks to the jury by asking them rhetorically whether they would be happy for a copy of the book to get into the hands of their daughter or one of their servants, a point which must have surprised most of the jury who didn't employ much below stairs. In a subsequent debate in the House of Lords on obscene publications one Peer, Lord Gage, referred to these remarks which were made during the Chatterley case:

I am not sure, my Lords, whether I would want my daughter to read this book,' he said. 'But I'm absolutely certain that I wouldn't want it to get into the hands of my gamekeeper.'